SLANT

ISBN: 979-834-3263787
Copyright©2024: Slow Lightning Lit
Printed in the United States of America
First Edition

All rights are reserved. No part of this book may be reproduced or transmitted in any form or by any means, electronic or mechanical, without the written permission of the Publisher except for educational purposes or in brief excerpts for promotion. For information: slowlightninglit@gmail.com.
*All rights herein are returned to their original authors after publication.

Editor-in-Chief
Peggy Dobreer, Slow Lightning Lit

Interior Format
Shannon Phillips, Picture Show Press

Website & Technical Assistance
Tiago Augusto Souza Barreiro

Guest Editor
Jeremy Ra

Consult
Nicelle Davis

Slow Lightning Press
uncommon works of poetry from uncommon writers
with a distinct vision for an uncommon book.

www.slowlightninglit.com

Slow Lightning Anthology III:

SLANT

Folio Edition

Introduction

Slow Lightning Lit III: SLANT, Folio Edition

This is a collection of **poetry folios** exploring themes of identity, fidelity, country, death, existential loss, mythic reflection and pure folly. They are poems written during unimaginably cruel human disasters, and even crueler political violence. They were written in relative privilege in a world vandalized by famine, suffering, and hate; a world making refugees instead of neighbors, building diaspora instead of villages. These are poems of inquiry and injury, reflections and confessions, whimsy and private moments. They include looking closely, looking away, looking back, and looking forward.

From many genres, cultures, and levels of experience these poets all share a strong sense of personal investigation, care of the other, investment in the craft of writing, and a largess of consideration beyond personal ego. They have each hit career highs in their respective fields that humble and inspire me.

Theses writers include long-time mentors, writing peers, mentees, and dearest friends—but you may have a hard time discerning which are which, as actually, all are all. I am deeply grateful for each of these fine writers, for the voices they are out in their own worlds, and for the voice of community and poetry that they raise together in this collection.

With abiding thanks to each Slow Lightning Lit contributor and associate, young, old, and ageless; to Janet Fitch for the initial inspiration for Slow Lightning meet-ups; to Lucien Zell for our name; to Bill Ratner and Tiago Augusto Souza Barreiro, who keep drawing cool maps and helping me follow them; and to you, dear readers who give this book legs.

Peggy Dobreer
Editor

Life is but a smile on the lips of death.
　　-Zhuang Zi, Warring States Period

Slow Lightning Lit: SLANT, Folio Edition

Table of Contents

Jacinta Camacho Kaplan..1
    Blasphemy
    Mercury Rising
    Twilight
    A Full House

Celia Chavez...7
    Low Autumn Light
    Winter Wardrobe
    Trainyard Love

Esther Cohen...13
    Life Story   Part I
    Life Story   Part II
    Life Story   Part III

Mandy Rae Hartz..19
    Disruptor: A Self Portrait
    Driving Forces
    Ever Wild

Loraine Despres 25
    My Problem
    What's the Point of Poetry
    Pirates

Peggy Dobreer...31
    Collateral
    4 Ablutions in Los Angeles
    Blue Ribbon

Darothy Durkac..37
> Proximity
> A Fabulist
> Where I Came From

Janet Fitch..43
> Insomnia
> Well, Thank God That's Over
> The Clever Curmudgeon
> The Mother Bone

Ruthie Marlenée 49
> Pheromones
> Catastrophic
> You're Pulling Away

Roberta Martínez 55
> Un Grano de Maiz
> Comadre
> Ports of Call

Murray Mednick 61
> False God
> The Rockers Sang Softly
> Crow

Andrew Nicholls...69
> A Wild Hypothetical
> With the Mrs.
> Down Shift

Colleen O'Mara Diamond 77
> My Next Life …
> Called to the Valley of the Moon
> When Leaves Fall Again

Simon Petty 83
> Morning Routine
> A Skein of Geese
> The Song Crows
> The Girl Who Learned to Speak Raven

Amy Raasch 91
> Vase with Poppies, 1886
> A Pair of Boots, 1887
> A Pair of Leather Clogs, 1888
> The Diggers, 1889

Bill Ratner 99
> The Collar
> Consecrated in Perugia
> Funeraria

Georgia San Li 107
> Jonquil
> Elegy for Fairy Wrens
> The Taxonomy of Being Desire
> The Smithsonian Book Dragon

June Stoddard 113
> My Action Figure
> Hideout
> Predominant Poise

Nancy Lynée Woo 119
> Signs of Life
> Self-Portrait with Clouds and Worry
> Listen

Guy Zimmerman 126
> The 68 Dreams of the Tantric Trucker
> An Equation
> Wake

Jacinta Camacho-KaplaN

Irreverence and humor are my cultural inheritance... In war and famine, peace and disaster... I deconstruct and reconstruct my world with poems. Boxes and crates of my poems await assembly into a book debut some year soon. It's important to have a safe space to poke at ideas that at first glance seem sacred.

Blasphemy

My anger swallows chili sauce as if it were breast milk.
hides in alleys and dark corners to stalk the almighty.

My anger swats at flies, steps on cockroaches, kills
spiders and eats snakes. Spits fire if you come too close.

Why are we such disappointing packages of flesh and
bone, failed creations, a bad experiment; no holy

mission obvious or sublime? Why are we so flawed,
so stupid, so shallow? Is that our misfortune,

or our great good luck to survive the mess we make?

Mercury Rising

Texas batted at the sun like Babe Ruth but entitled.
More heat, more heat, more heat, the state shouted,
*melt fish, sand crabs, turtles and those damn migrants
at the border. Seize those freed slaves, and those too
obvious Asians who think a hyphen followed by American
is a sanctuary. Get rid of anyone not Baptist, the right
kind of Baptist in this 110 degree clime.*

Texas sweat is pure if you are Texan, the most desirable
sweat in the whole country to empower purebred Texans.
Greed is the state's creed.

What is Texas; country like Hungary but bigger, more
autocratic with a ballot box; like Italy under Mussolini;
like Russia under Putin? Who votes in Texas; heat exhausted
men and women; starving for shade, clean water, a near-by
food bank; and a ballot box?

Twilight

We drank Campari with apricot nectar
    On our hotel balcony overlooking Portofino.
We celebrated the longest day
    Of our long marriage.

This summer tonic layered its sunset
    in pomegranate and peach, not the purple
hues of unavoidable sorrows. We held
    time as sacred, a gift.

Room service pasta may not have been
    the finest available but it was the best for
us that day. The longest day, the last longest
    day we would practice together.

Love lived here with all the misunder-
    standings and mundane chaos married life
brings. And children, yes, all four. The hours
    talking in bed, reading our letters to each
other, touching till we fell asleep.

A Full House

what house will I die in? what house will choose me?
what forest? what garden? what room will I prefer to
die in? what book will I read? what song will I sing or
listen to? how much longer do I have? days, hours,
minutes? what have I forgotten to finish or do? have I
lived well enough, loved enough, listened enough?
do I understand what my life means? how many mistakes
were only mine? who did I deceive, betray, leave? who?
why? when? is forgiveness possible? am I capable
of forgiveness? am I remorseful? what's left to know?

Celia ChaveZ

Celia Chavez credits Slow Lightning for redemption from volumes of jejune verse recently excavated from her mother's house. She returns to poetry through songwriting, with a desire to synthesize her Filipina-American heritage, coast to coast moves, and globetrotting life as a pro singer in booty shorts. She is Babilonia (her solo music persona), Womancake Magazine's music editor, and was long-listed for the 2024 Fish Poetry Prize.

Low Autumn Light

Look at the low autumn light through the leaves I say.
In the quiet of being thousands of miles removed
from rockets and blood, leaves turn color and fall.
My mind drifts to my grandfather's blood running out
into the street as invaders took his house
and our family fled, refugees into jungle hills.

The lake is almost frozen over, I remark
in the hushed tones of someone separated
by oceans and continents from snipers and shells.
Your mother tells me she never learned to ski as a girl,
there were no mountains in the country where her parents
sent her to escape the bombing blitz back home.

Little Annie throws seed at a flotilla of ducks.
They come ashore to chase her bright-colored coat,
her bobblehead hat. She squeals and runs to the woods
to hide-and-seek. This far north, her father and mother
and you and me unravel the morning glory vines of war
so she can skip through the dappled light between trees.

I follow her to collect each sliver of wonder,
each stripe on a firecrest's head,
every rainbow combination,
every ruby red rose she sees.

Winter Wardrobe

Say goodbye to winter
open the spare suitcase
in the back of the closet
throw in a lavender sachet

Pile in all the sweaters
and coats of protective down
the faithless fabric I wrap myself in
when I forget a sky beyond clouds

I brace for the long night
pinprick dreams beneath
a snow-blanket hush
that masks my impatient doubt

I'm a January amnesiac
carousel seasons still circle
while frozen ground drowns out
the rustling energy of bulbs

Today is dry and balmy
for bare arms and cropped pants
naked ankles flash the sun
eyeshades dare the noontime glare

Seeds stockpile color for release
timed perfectly with rising mercury
and the mating dances of birds
building new nests in the sky

Trainyard Love

How can softness stop a bullet
    or halt an army's march?
    Love is wrapped in a white flag

I want Kevlar love
    that keeps cruelty behind barbed wire
    a firearm on each hip

I want soldier love
    that scouts ahead for danger
    heads it off sniper-like from higher ground

I want hard rock love
    headbanging to a twisted
    derivative of the blues

I want linebacker love
    faster than a freight train of trouble
    to headbutt any harm headed for me

But I need vagabond love
    to run alongside me in the trainyard
    to warm its hands in fingerless gloves
    with me at a trash can campfire

    Shelter me with a shrug of shoulders
    Throw one arm around me

Esther CoheN

Esther Cohen is one of thousands of Esther Cohens. Like many of them, she lives in New York City. She writes a poem every single day.

Life Story

1

When I was born

my father, a Talmudic man

who didn't think he'd marry

didn't think he'd have children,

my father, celebrated my birth

by buying a large green beach house

for two families with

his college roommate, Solly.

Solly was an inventor.   His most

noteworthy invention: a device

for restaurant bathrooms that could

dry hands by pressing a button.

No towels were involved.

For many summers, my family

father mother brother and me

lived in that house. We were all

happiest right there.

(Not so Solly, whose wife Elaine,

thinner than the rest of us,

declared our house was nowhere.

Not only that, Elaine said.

Our neighbors were not

people of note. They moved

to Westchester and we

never saw any of them again.

2

Abby was my best friend

at the beach. We spent

all our days together.

Our mothers

were good friends too.

My mother was Sara.

Abby's was Bess.

Bess ironed and ironed.

Sara never ironed a thing.

We made a newsletter

together called Gab.

I wrote the stories, and Abby

illustrated them. Most

of the stories were embellished

descriptions of our neighbor

Joanie Mendlestein's dating life.

We devoted six pages, our

longest issue ever to

Joanie's engagement

to Howard. Years later,

we both moved

to New York City. Abby

became a successful photographer.

We'd have dinner at least

once a year. Mostly, we'd discuss

Sara and Bess, both infinite

subject matter. Abby suddenly

died this summer.

I can't believe she's gone.

3

After Bess died in Florida,

Abby and I had a very long dinner

Abby brought two artifacts

back home for our dinner:

Bess's Metamucil bottle

which she'd used for a martini shaker

and a small tightly wrapped box

which Abby hoped contained

a secret – something unfathomable

that Bess kept hidden. She'd

found the box in Bess's nightstand drawer.

Our best guess was an electric dildo.

Abby brought scissors and

razor blades to undo

the wrapping at dinner. She

was careful to take off the wrapping

just in case. Neither of us

could have guessed what

was inside: A plaster cast

with an index card: Bunion

from Bess Glazer's left foot.

We couldn't believe it.

Mandy Rae HartZ

Whether writing poetry, parenting our two Love Nuggets, or organizing for the greater good, I take the same approach: With a hopeful heart and always on the edge of tears, dive in! I came to Slow Lightening after a period of midlife excavation and the realization that while poetry breathes at the core of my being, I'd kept the practice safely on the outskirts of my priority list. Until now. In this community, I'm rediscovering the joy of creating, the awe of humanity, and — most powerfully — me.

Disruptor: A Self Portrait

Like a riot of desert poppies
announce the strike of Spring
microdoses of electric adrenaline
buzz and burst
beneath my skin.

Excitement and anxiety
physiologically
all the same,
but the experiential difference
drives values fired change.

I line my lips vampire red
and remember little me:
Standing tiptoe atop an overturned milkcrate
ponytail, braces, blue jeans
peering over the podium
transformed
by seeing
and being seen.

Future, present, and past collapse
each time I take the stage.
Watch my mouth.
Listen now.
Our mission calls for courage.

Darlings, we will remember
this collective hopeful current;
even if
we all forget
these channeled tinderbox words.

Driving Forces (Milo)

The son of a Disruptor
(his mother, that's me)
he was born for this world
to drive change.

Milo makes no proposals,
knows only demands.
Feels the biggest of feelings,
takes the grandest of stands.

He rarely sees need
for asking permission,
sets his own limits
with grit and intuition.

In him my own mother's
wishes came true:
I got one just like me
(and just like her, too).

But this difference between us
(and this one's enough):
Knowing "too much"
is so easy to love.

Ever Wild

This birthday wish
for my own sweet child:
May you feel ever loved
and stay ever wild.

Grow too big for your britches.
Decide for yourself where's your place.
Treat yours and all souls with kindness.
With grace embrace your mistakes.

Love hard.
Eat slowly.
Rest often.

Do it with joy, whatever you do.

Shine brightly.
Read nightly.
And take every chance to howl at the moon.

Loraine DespreS

Loraine Despres is a storyteller. Her novels include The Scandalous Summer of Sissy LeBlanc, now in its 22nd printing, and The Bad Behavior of Belle Cantrell. She wrote many television shows but is best remembered for "Who Done It?" known worldwide as the "Who Shot J.R.?" episode of DALLAS. She came to poetry to polish her prose but instead fell down the rabbit hole of verse from which she has never emerged.

My
Problem

When you tell me

your problem as you

would because we're friends

or even if you don't, especially if

you don't, and I can see you see you

suffer because we're friends after all and

I want to lend a helping hand and make your

problem my problem even if you haven't, maybe

especially if you haven't asked me to do anything. My

brain goes into firefighting mode. It's then I enthusiastically,

oh, so enthusiastically lay out all the things that you should do,

you should do because I care about you, and have given your problem

so much thought. So, I press, and I press until you do what you must do

and tell me to shut up.

What's the Point of Poetry

It flutters and flies around my room, knocking against

the windowpanes in short stanzas. It's the Tic Toc

of literature. From preparation through insemi-

nation to culmination is usually just a slip

of time. It's a song with unsung music.

Hard to grasp as a summer breeze

circling softly around the ceiling.

But sometimes, a poem bur-

rows deep into your body

until it's keeping time to

the flow of your blood

as it enters and

leaves your

heart.

Pirates

The little girl, in a pink nightgown, sits

cross legged on top of her white pillow

which has turned into a raft on a billowing white

sea where wrinkles have become waves. It's after 8:00

and even though she's not a bit sleepy, her hard-hearted

parents have banished her from the grownup gossip

and laughter and clink of ice in cocktail glasses in

the living room where the living people are. She

uncrosses her legs and crosses them again left over right

and nods to her older brother, who may be imaginary but

who's always ready for adventure. They are shipwrecked

once again on their white pillow raft. Across the room,

near the floor she spots a light. A boat on the horizon?

She turns to him. "What do you think? Are they friends

or pirates?" He hands her an imaginary brass spyglass.

She makes an open fist, holds it to her eye and sees a

skull and crossbones. "Pirates again! Just like last

night!" she cries, bouncing on the springing waves.

Decades later after working with real pirates,

she finds herself kidnapped, pirated away but

now she's locked in her mind, banished again

from the living room where adults laugh

over stories she no longer understands.

Peggy DobreeR

Peggy Dobreer is a multiple Pushcart nominated poet with three published collections. A former dancer and lifelong student of mystical traditions, she is a builder of incubators and community spaces; a lab rat exploring generative, experiential modalities. A former guest teacher at AEE, WITS, and AROHO2015, she is curator of Slow Lightning Lit's daily somatic practice, out of which 'uncommon' publishing and literary events are imagined.

Collateral

The sweetness of clementine grass
                      mimics the scent of grail.
There are more questionable gods and
                      unrequited goddesses
in this poem than I have ever read in
                      wartime. Under siege
any mention of food during famine
                      or home during exodus
seems another subtle aggression. So, I write
                      larks in a clementine coven,
wings averting weather, eyes looking past clouds.
                      I write lovers in a battered afterward,
stroke my cheeks with copycat verse and imagine
                      that the unidentified caller rings
to bring a mitzvah for the tired, and preening.
                      Meanwhile, a gilded wealth
of western sky at sunset, a cup of warm
                      Palo Azul with an easy
twist of nevermore, waiting for little
                      or nothing at all.

4 Ablutions (Greater Los Angeles)

1. Robaire's

A shiny bowl of lemon water
At a white linen covered table.
A man in a trimmed goatee
Demonstrates with a wink.
Stands nearby with a towel.
Two trains of thought collide
At these pristine and sterling
Rituals for snails drenched
In truffle butter, which up
To this point were creatures
Only known to me in mud.

2. Wilshire District

A large basin in the marble foyer
of Mr. Slotnikov's eldest daughter.
All the mirrors along the stairwell
draped in black cloth like the skirt
around a coffin during viewing.
Lox and bagels waited on ice.
Dishes of cream cheese, capers,
green olives, purple onions, and
White Herring. All the colors
of mourning. Nobody had eaten
much of anything for three days
but none of us was quite ready
to swallow any of this just yet.

3. Echo Park

In a brand spanking new hillbilly
hot tub on Harvey's back porch
under a giant Eucalyptus trying
luckless to blot out the moon

I lay back with a pink Barbie inner
tube beneath my head, a hose from
the laundry room to the trough,
which Harvey augmented with
hot water from buckets on the stove.

A caterer for many years, he always
tended to finishing touches. Steam
rose with the scent of Eucalyptus
and a sprig of homegrown rosemary
he slipped into every pouring.

4. Bloomingdales

Maneuvering from task to task she stopped
and stepped outside. A hot drizzle started
to stain the deck in sizeable polka dots.
A palpable petrichor calling her to herself,
she clasped her hands behind her bottom,
chest open, long, deep breaths. Lips ajar,
she drank from the goblet of sky, reached
her arms out to catch a few drops, then
noticed her silk sleeves puckering. She
had carried that fine haberdashery
on her credit card for months. And still
she stood there and let the rain ruin her.

Blue Ribbon

We might be here till the cow slips
over the edge of the Hunter's Moon,
till the rings of Saturn dissolve
like cotton candy in a warm drizzle.

The county fairgrounds are muggy,
damp hay and sawdust, all shit-kick and
corn-on-the-cob with moist BBQ. I
came dressed in red and white gingham,

thinking of sunshine, straw hats, square
dance and homemade pies. People like
to show you up at the fairgrounds. That active
Americana, competitive spirit in every booth,

riding the bulls, frying up the best fritters,
quilting, or raising the finest sow in the crowd.
Our family never did the fair, my urban stepdad
opposed to dust, and any random collection

of the unsanitized public. He did take me
to see Marcel Marceau the year the Music
Center first opened. I could have sworn
a glass box existed at the center of that stage.
I've always had a knack for seeing what isn't there.

Darothy DurkaC

Poetry entices me daily in SL meditation. The embodied lines that appear are a diagnostic of my will and sentience. My micro fiction, "What He Did With the Inside" rewarded me with a stay in Lismore, Ireland, and, "The Map" was long listed for Fish Publishing. Listening to and reading poetry brings me into the present, and reassembles some sense of this world.

Proximity

Rachel told me never to question things.
Not the fat, yellow slugs on her tomato plants
worthy of admiration climbing so high,
only to be plucked off.

Nor us spending summer days in her room,
emerging at sunset to take photos of our shadows.
Not of us, she insisted.

I'll braid your hair, you braid mine.
We'll pile them on top of our heads,
like cake.
I twisted her vines round my fingers like Jacob's Ladder.

No need for me to question her lack of hunger.
Why aren't you eating? I'd ask.
I see too much. And hardboiled eggs are shy.
So, we refused her mother's food and picked berries from a bush.

Don't worry, she wrote to me from the nuthouse
where she was often sent,
You can make it over the playground rail,
just swing higher, let go of the chains.

She returned, assured me about the color of darkness.
No, it's like a mushroom, or dog hair,
or my beauty mark,
as she held the brush and stroked her walls black.

A Fabulist

On pace he filled his pipe.
    His words held me in place.
A backbeat from the washing machine chugged,
        steady as drumsticks on rocks, or clay.
My mother stood aware.

His mud was the battle of Somme,
        a soft word for agony.
Somme, inked on the honorable discharge papers
    my mother kept for him.

How is honor made? No complaints, no regrets?
    I craved more than his arrival/departure from that French river town.
His eyes stared at the street, go on, I pleaded. Excavate.

He fabled his comings and goings: Cuba, Algiers, New York.
      We fabled ourselves
through plumes of pipe smoke,
    and chocolate squares, his gift to me like his words
I nibbled.

At fables end he always took the last bus home to downtown LA
    in fedora and grease-stained suit,
to the Spring Street Hotel
    third floor, high enough.

Where I Came From

I come from two lovers, who left New York for the West,
and thought it was paradise, at first.
A mother accustomed to small portions,
I found myself perpetually hungry.
A father with an appetite for beef and tomatoes,
craved gravy with the meal.
He and I ate toast at night to stave off our hunger.

With her I walked the village perimeter,
heard Warblers and Flickers, smelled lilacs, watched clouds.
I longed to see what she saw in the distance, there,
on the bus to Sears, in her reading chair, at the dinner table.

With him each week, we went to the movies:
Z, Satyricon, Bonnie and Clyde. So many I wish
I remember them all.
He never asked me to cover my eyes, or tried
to explain what we'd seen.

They gave me roller skates, jeans, a bike,
things they'd never had.
They took me to grape boycotts, and precinct walks
with shouts to end the war.
On their bookshelves I found and read Vietnam! Vietnam!, Hiroshima,
Henry Miller.

In tire-soled sandals, I galloped through the canyon
chapparal and scrub, yarrow and sumac,
on my way to Will Rogers Beach,
where I dozed on the sand, for hours.

I learned how our paradise dressed herself in succulent layers,
disguised violence and hate, too late.

Janet FitcH

I came to poetry through my novels. I wrote the poems of Ingrid Magnussen in *White Oleander*, and those of Marina Makarova and other fictional poets, in *The Revolution of Marina M.* and *Chimes of a Lost Cathedral*. Poetry echoes in *Paint It Black*. It was only after finishing these novels that I began writing poems in my own voice.

Insomnia

    –for James Merrill

What women do at 3 a.m.
When worry like a corkscrew
Propels them from their beds.

They talk to the cat.

Catch up on emails to friends
in Australia or Japan.
Wash dishes forgotten at bedtime.

They read something quiet—no crime, God forbid.
Bludgeon isn't a word for this time of night.
It's a time for companionable poets.

I like James Merrill now.
Sitting with that sanity.
He has his problems too

But that's not the point.
He teases apart the mysteries
He's right there with you..

By five you're asleep on the couch
The cat comes to sleep with you
As he's usually not allowed,
the bedroom door shut tight.

And Merrill's face gazes
from the spine of his fat book.
We never run out
Of poems, or nights.

Well, Thank God That's Over

The wall
    You've been pushing on
        Falls away at last
And you find
    You don't know
        How to stand anymore

Death after long illness.
    Divorce that comes at last.
        Armistice Day.

At the parade of the wounded
    the veteran sits on his doorstep
        limp flag in hand.

The move from the dump
    you managed to raise your kids in.
        Good riddance!

Thank God that's over.

You hold the Hot Wheel
    found loose in an old drawer,
        the beaded hair tie.

And find yourself weeping.
    Not so easy
        as you thought it would be.

The Clever Curmudgeon

Two old ladies on a park bench
In any city in the world
Passing judgement on the parade.

The grumpy one with the jaundiced eye,
Funny and razored.
And the sunny one, assuming the best.

The clever curmudgeon
Believes the other's an idiot.
They've been friends sixty years,
She should know.

My grandmother, taking in
Some fashion eyepopper
Would say,
'Now there's a look.'

The universe laughs
All day long.

They say
One eye is the mercy eye,
The other's for judgement.

Clever's gotten me through days
I might have offed myself.
But God, I'm so tired of her.
Could I wear an eyepatch?

Now there's a look.

The Mother Bone

Antlers grew out of my head
    First a little stub
    Then a second branch
      Soon
          A candelabra of bone
          Rose from my head
          Like a forest

A woman with antlers
    must walk slow
    and very upright
    else she will topple
    or snag.

Am I to lower my head
and butt with a clang
    another antlered being?
They're more like antennae
    channeling messages
        dripping with dew

The stag walks silent
through the mist and
knee-high ferns
the cathedral forest
already crowned.

    Meaning clings to my antlers
    Drips down the branches like
    the dew.
        Not quite human
        after all.

Ruthie MarlenéE

Ruthie Marlenée is the Mexican-American author of *Agave Blues, Isabela's Island,* and *Curse of the Ninth.* She is at work on the sequel *And Still Her Voice.* A Pushcart nominee, Marlenée's poetry can be found in S*low Lightning: Impractical Poetry* and *Astonished Poetry.* Ruthie is known to believe in the power of family, true love, and tequila.

Pheromones

When the pheromones hit, I was
at an intersection, window rolled down
I felt his eyes sizzle into my ear.
His engine revved. I tried to back up
but the signal changed from yellow
to red, hot and bothered,
and then to green. A race!

When the pheromones hit
I was in the aisle at the grocery store.
His hand brushed mine
as we reached for tomato sauce.
Spaghetti tonight? he asks,
my face burning and turning
the shade of marinara.

When the pheromones hit
I was in the audience
at my daughter's piano recital.
He took the seat next to me.
Do you play? he whispered.
Oh, wouldn't you like to tickle my ivories?
or *We could play a wild duet.*

Looking straight, I sat on my hands
swallowed and then answered,
I haven't for a very long time.

Catastrophic

    —after Martha Silano

I wondered if unscrambling "melanoma"
might yield me a lemon to make lemonade?
Or maybe I'd just be squeezed out and left
alone to moan -- a "melan"choly party of one.

If I were to unscramble "melanoma"
would it become a lame omen?
Would I learn that you're just on loan
until our last lean meal together?

If "melanoma" had been unscrambled sooner
would there have been a balm-like aloe
to soothe the suspicious mole on your face?
Would the memo on metastasis be suspended?

Unscrambling "melanoma", will I find the ammo
to end this personal Battle of the Alamo?
Can the mean ole tumors, like exploding
ammonal, be stopped from colonizing?

Now, as I unscramble "melanoma"
all I see is a name for I love – amo –
Te amo. I love you,
the salve to my alma, the mate to my soul!

And, what if I unscramble "melanoma"
and scream it away with the two letters – NO!
Can I just pray to God, and Mama, and all heaven's
angels to please heal my man? Can I get an AMEN?

You're Pulling Away

I see it in the smile, unmatched
by eyes stuck like distant duds for stars
never coming close anymore, the dazzling
doused by tears you will not spare,
emotions you will no longer share.

You're pulling away from me
I feel it in fleeting fingers, icy hands
that no longer linger long enough
to squeeze my wilting cheeks
neither top nor bottom
I know it's nothing I have caused
nothing you can control
The doctors are working on a cure

You're pulling away from me
and hope, a damaged buoy struggling
to stay afloat, sinks down like a rock
Oh my rock, my lifesaver, my port in the storm
You've shown me a love without bounds
without conditions, a love that is not a mirage
In you I believed all things possible.
I've traveled far, gone deep, conquered
heights, navigated life's twists and turns
but only as Miss Daisy with you at the wheel

You're pulling away from me.
Pushing into yourself to save me, to spare me
prepare me for the day you leave me
to find my reading glasses on my head
to figure things out on my own
like how to make the perfect cup of coffee
with a swirl of whipped crème
I'll figure out which pills are for mourning
which pills are for night.

Roberta H. Martínez

I'm a Chicana who grew up in East Los and keeps going back to places where the tortillas are fresh and the jamaica is just a little tart. Colors and textures dance and have movement for those who work in the plastic and visual arts. Stories in playwriting, poetry, and pose do the same for me. They are born of my feelings and thoughts on the thousand little stories we share with each other sometimes in a look, other times in a touch, and yet other times, enclosed in a whisper.

Un Grano de Maíz

I see the grain that fed us
I remember the sound of chachayotes and penacho's rustling
Danzantes embracing ancient meters, dust lifted by dance
I smell the Copal, purifying; its smoke slowly rising
I remember
Mine were the gente who changed the dirt to soil
So that maíz would rise tall, their roots, like talons
Stretching and growing over rocks
Tassels rustling, telling us when it's time
In a single grain of maíz
I know
That my roots are theirs
Their stories, my stories, are my strength
That in the sharing of our stories
We plant the seeds of strength for our children

Comadres P/V*

My comadre always wore makeup
She wouldn't leave home without it
She lived in a house on a hill that could see
From City Terrace to the Long Beach lights
She was the holder of words I didn't connect with me
Elegant, voluptuous, scandalous, glamour driven
Her eyes could smolder or laugh or cry
Her mouth was the sort for which deep colored lipstick was created
The small of her back was immortalized for the world to see: **forever
La Tormenta**
Her shoes were almost always high heeled and fashion present
She introduced me to Ferlinghetti
She never embraced my Emily
I preferred braids or Pixie cut Jeans to satin or chiffon
Unless the chiffon was a very twirly skirt
It was her laugh that drew me to her
Our shared knowledge of screwball comedy
And the images our TVs gave us in black and white
That tethered us to each other
The comfort in not being in competition with each other
Of sisterhood
Of my being her emotional doula at her daughter's birth
Of her being Our Lady of the Eyeliner on my daughter's prom night
Ever each other's flying buttress
Even to this day

*Por vida

Ports of Call

He woke up that morning and the hot air reminded him
Drink a lot of water today
The sun was strong on his tent, and he could hear the voices outside
Words darting this way and that
In English, in Arabic
And he heard himself thinking in Polish
How long had it been since he'd heard his mother tongue here
How long had it been since he had heard his mother's voice
Or tasted her pierogies
And a memory like a bit of ash
Floated about
A memory of an Easter morning
Pysanky placed on table
The eggs transformed by lines and leaf patterns
A mix of modern and old-fashioned designs
And the smell of kielbasa and ham
And the sweet memory of the perfume of onions made him smile
Pot and spoon, and sizzle sound
Sigh…
He dressed, ate a protein bar, and jumped in the van
He was still smiling when the missile hit the van
And the food they were carrying
The food they were going to give with love
Became indistinct bits of metal and flesh and hope
And for a time, hate was greater than love

Murray MednicK

Murray Mednick is best known as the founder of the Padua Playwrights Workshop and Festival; or perhaps for the Obie Award for his play, *The Deer Kill;* or perhaps for a lifetime of award winning plays in publication with Padua Press. Starting out as a young poet with the beats in NYC, Mednick did not take to reading his own poetry. A career of writing verse for the stage was an excellent solution to that dilemma.

False God

I think he is reincarnated like an old soul.
Motherfucker belongs high up in the sky
Above the atmosphere, above the clouds,
Where no birds sing, where Nothing is,
No air to breathe, no screaming or hitting
Or lying, or suffering, or seeing one's own
Bullshit over and over. I'd like to look
Up to him, up there where nothing is and
Nothing does, away, away from that
Power banging old and angry white fat
Con and his stupefied followers arming
As we speak, preparing to attack, to kill
Me and my kind here on planet earth,
A satellite of the Sun, dying of its own
Accord, a systematic unraveling of
Its skin, down to the bare storming fire
In its Center, Iron, hot as the sun. If only
I could stop the constant chatter and just
Be. But that's not what's up. What's up
Is the astounding chaos, inside and out,
On the street, in the power lines, in the gut,
The sound of an army of insects clamoring
And fighting for the space to breathe. Not
Strictly iambic, more the pounding of a dactylic
Torrent, fire and flood, murder and War.

The Rockers Sang Softly

The rockers sang softly as we approached the Sun,
Strumming their guitars like avatars,
Confident and exposed, as only humans are,
Their faces and voices like the movie
Images of what they finally are –
Stuck in bodies, returning to elements
Like slowly dying, exploding stars, which is
What they are, what they are –
Brief expressions of a dying star.

Subconsciously,
I have invented a doppelganger –
She sleeps with me and is there when I wake.
First thing as I stir, is to be sure
She is there with me in my bed,
Is pleased, is glad to be there,
Independent of race, or task,
Or obligation, as we are, as we are.
But then she wakes and calls me names
And then she's gone, a mist remains.

Another death today – sorrow seeps in
Like an old leak – hardly knew the woman.
Didn't like me for some reason,
Or we didn't hit it off, as they used to say.
I see her fading now into memory,
Her sound and image wasting away.
"Sally" seemed inappropriate,
So she renamed herself "Alexandra."
May the theater gods protect her.

A book in the mail from two old friends.
One, the poems, the other, the drawings.
In the intro, some idiot ascribed to me a quote.
A Wise Guy saying things.

(I was so pleased to be mentioned.)
But then I got angry. Finally read the poems.
Same old good abstract stuff.
Now it's another loss for me, misquoted
45 years ago, and again. More losses,
all the way back to Brooklyn College.

Where do I stand because of paranoia
And insecurity? Fragments of emotion
In awkward abstract places.
"Maybe he didn't get the message.
Maybe you never sent the message.
Maybe he misunderstood the message.
Stupid to send a message in the first place."
There my father sits in a 1943 photo –
Cracked and slightly unhinged.
I was four years old at the time.

People losing their memory, then their lives.
Most of the time, I don't feel anything.
My sister looked like the dark Jewesses
Of old, ancient, facing the sunrise
When she passed, at peace, but
Disappointed. I kept her company.
Soon, I scattered her ashes over Prospect Park.
Babies will breathe her ashes.
Maybe you'll get a chance to see me –
that moment as I sit up painfully.

Talent: like shackles of a gold chain.
I still have hopes of forgiveness
From the universe, the deep sky.
A true warrior's death.
Without fear or shame,
Matt, sitting in the sunrise.

You don't get a chance to go back,
Fix it up. Even The sages were confounded:

Either they went somewhere or not.
Is it totally up to you?
Get your feet washed and clean.
Do your children know right from wrong?
How to think? Make the signs to an invisible God?
And if you have a half a brain,
Write something down, say a poem, fall to your knees.

Looking ahead, straight into the wilderness, s not pleasant.
You are running for your life,
Your heart's not in it,
Fall back with the tribe, with the living, the young.
It was a Catskill joke
By Jack Benny, who didn't laugh.
He never laughed, deadpan forever.
I think of my mother and "I love Lucy"
As I run. The woman is dangerous
And she's got RED lipstick on her mouth.
Fuck this shit. Run.

Wrong, I must have done something wrong.
How could I be so caught?
Because God himself had a personal hatred for my mother,
And we were consigned to Hell for Eternity.
We were and are of the pariah class.
And not only that, but I was her only defense.
Now you're going to get it, she used to say,
You scum of the lower classes,
Abandoning your mother for your father.

Her own family had abandoned her
And now she had to fend off debts
And my father's never-ending sexual demands.
"No, not tonight, Sol,
And maybe never ha, ha, ha."
"Did you pay the goddamned electricity?"
He'd say, wanting to knock her head off.
"Where's the money, Sol, to pay?"

"It's up your ass," he'd say, "it's up your ass."

I have a picture of my father
Which may not be him,
He could be another uncle, but I think it's him,
Good looking guy with the dog,
In the cold, in the Catskills,
I don't know why I think it's him –
The good-natured, best-looking, smilingly
Dumb teenager – I'll frame it
And put it up next to my soccer photo.

I'm a senior in high school and the captain
Sitting in the center with the ball,
The best-looking guy on the team, smiling
In my glory like my dad,
The center of attention,
I was cadging lunches with ease at the time,
You can't tell if the kid's anxious or not,
The captain of the soccer team,
And the darkest and handsomest by far.

I'm old and alone and less than handsome now.
I've forgotten the vanity of good looks.
Totally gone from my life.
In those days it both surprised and encouraged me.
Having that beautiful face
I didn't know what any of it meant.
I'm not sure I do know now.

Crows

Another poem about crows. Listening
To crows, watching crows, fighting crows,
Crow dog and his pack of crows,
Be there with the crows,
Documenting a moment in
The Valley with the crows
And the beloved trees,
Orange and figs, pomelo, avocado,
And the flowers, the quiet houses,
No way to preserve the life in me
Here, the sky, the trees, the silence.

Andrew Nicholls

Andrew Nicholls wrote his first poem, "Bleep and Booster Go To The Moon," at the age of six, for his family. It did not reach a wider audience. He focusses mostly on humor, for television, print and stage.

A Wild Hypothetical

If they scatter

        the ground-
up bits

    of a person — say, you

or your sister

       in a field, or, say,

along a one-mile strip of highway
    and I'm talking the whole body here,
        hair to toenails, mulched
then randomly

    distributed,

that's important,

so the knees aren't necessarily
    below the waist (or what had
        been the waist,

or pieces

       of the waist)

of your sister or of you;

so that what-

    had-been-you

or your sister could now be said to lie

entirely on that mile of highway – and
    if, when you were alive,
        (after you, or your sister,

encountered

    this poem

but before,

    obviously,

you were mulched) you
    crossed that highway barefoot,
        within this one-mile stretch...

would the parts

    of you or

your sister

    – eyes, ears,

brain cells –
    that are

absorbing these words right now
    possibly touch the parts of you
        (i.e. the skin of your feet)

that walked you

    or your sister

across

    the highway

towards the destiny wherein you were
    (presumably unpleasantly)
        later mulched?

and if so,

    did this poem

warning

    you or your sister

Just not work?

Maybe you should call her.

With the Mrs.

When inculcating tender minds
    In tongues obtuse and foreign
I recommend a trick by which
    Philologists have sworeign:
A *bon mot* here, a *mot juste* there
    Dispersed throughout your parlance
Will give your young a well-deserved
    Head start, the little darlance.

So, come child, sit on the souvenir
    And let me look at you
Put a concierge in your buttonhole
    And stroll the parvenu
You look like a milieu bucks tonight –
    There's a rapport at the door!
Remember the à la mode my dear
    And be home by cordial to four.

You're crying – have you quatre yourself?
    Aren't you old enough to lorgnette?
Let me look at it under the magnifique –
    Put a badinage uporgnette
To bed, to beddikins little one...
    Now I'm alone with the Mrs.
"Adieu anything special in mind?"
    "Oh, panache me with krs!"

Let's take a cab for a midnight ride,
    The moon is so éclair
Or better yet, let's take my car
    And save the savoir-faire.
Returning home, we'll plan a trip
    To Paris, Cannes or Ypres
Then light a great big bonsoir
    And talk ourselves to slypres.

Down Shift

In the spring a young man's

                fancy meeting you here

I'm afraid you leave me no

                choice cuts of beef

I'm glad that he got his

                comeuppance see me any time

It's clear that kid's got what

                It takes a thief.

There's more to this than

                Meets Me in St. Louis.

The sun

                A rose by any other name

It isn't if you win or lose, it's

                Howdy Doody time.

  Your mother just

                Called on account of rain.

Colleen O'Mara DiamonD

A writer of stories, essays and poetry, Colleen lives and works in beautiful, emerging Ojai, California. She manages an international communications agency and her book projects include a debut memoir titled *Raw Diamond*. Colleen's work has been published in the *Los Angeles Times*, *Urban Howl*, *Slow Lightning II: Astonished Poetry*, and the *Northridge Review*. She was short-listed by Fish Publishing for memoir.

My Next Life

In my next life

      I am going to be late

                for dinner
  appointments

late

    to my own wedding

                and funeral

I am going to be

light

    flaky

        irresponsible

     iridescent

Wear tutu skirts

    and cocktail dresses

             to meetings
Yoga pants

              to black-tie affairs

Wooly winter sweaters

      in August

  Sleeveless cotton dresses

     for December

       Follow no rules

      regulations

     guidelines

    Agree to no

   Guardrails

I will say things like

  May be

   Could be

    I don't know

     People won't even try to box me in

   They will give up shrug shoulders purse lips

Know that I am a black shiny slick raincoat   Nothing sticks.

When Leaves Fall Again

He makes images magically dance across a film or television screen.
His first wife, my friend, fell ill and passed into the stars.
She visits now -- a Monarch Butterfly -- in the garden.
From off the kitchen floor, I picked up his pieces, his mosaic's tesserae,
Filled the gaps in grout mixed with patience.
We gathered our three little ones between us, and filled picnic
Baskets full of fun -- to parks, museums, beaches -- long, dusty road
Trips around our beloved California.
In between the joy and laughter of adventure we fell in love.
Seven years ago this November, when the red and orange leaves fall again
Another page of our calendar will turn.

Called to the Valley of the Moon ...

the house fell from the sky
after a three-year search.

Summer 2017
baked the earth so hot,
it brought fire at Christmas time.
Burned a circle around downtown,
and left the white arches of the Arcade untouched.

Fire is a purifier,
a sign of renewal.
It seared our past
in the city to the south by the sea.
Brought us to oak trees with pointy leaves that poke fingertips.
Moon so bright, like daylight,
it throws shadows on the gravel.
Stars spread out, a celestial blanket above.

Turkey vultures circle, wing spans vast and beaks curious.
"Pink Moments" when the sun sets, and
the Topa Topa Mountains' face glows.

A Hawk perches on a lonely tree branch
above the bungalow, a Craftsman.
She mistakes the dog for a rabbit or ground squirrel.
Lands on the weathered fence,
turns her head from side to side.
She whispers to me — a good omen.

The Ventura River sits at the end of our road,
curves and swirls,
expands for the storms' rains,
widens to make room for the new water.
It overflows now,
like my heart.

Simon PettY

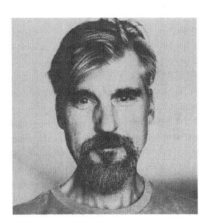

Simon Petty is studying for his MFA in Creative Writing at Antioch University. He was shortlisted for the Bridport Prize in 2020 and the Fish Poetry Prize in 2024. He writes, plays, and teaches music in Los Angeles with his partner, Celia Chavez.

Morning Routine

Ground your feet

grind the beans

grin and bear it

through the headline grief

greet the unwelcome dawn.

On the other side of daybreak,

wings dry on a concrete porch in the winter sun,

clouds shadow in the middle distance,

a soft old dog is carried down an apartment stairwell:

everything is suddenly expanding and

too close at the same time.

The heart breaks

and mends,

incrementally.

A Skein of Geese

I've played so many
brides down the aisle
Palm Springs processionals,
golf course sincerity.
It's not for them that I sing.
I play for the bats and the nightjars
the flicker of wings at the edge of the light.

Wine bottles sweat in silver buckets, unopened.
It's unlucky to toast with water
the best man whispers
sotto voce
What does he know of this?

I look up at the circle of sky:
a skein of geese in a flying V
heads towards Greenland.

Above the mountain skyline
the lights of a nighttime jet
briefly intersect with Orion's belt
to sew the three stars together
in an absurd coincidence
of old light and optical nerves.

It feels as if it signifies
something I will never comprehend,
but I'm here
I know I
saw it happen.

The Song Crows

They found three more
the other day, in an office
just off Soho Square, discarded
long before the millennium.

The song crows are calling to me
wailing from the Underworld
Why did you not take care of me?
Why did you leave?

They wisp and crowd around my skull,
ear worms burrow,
taglines snag.
They won't let me be.

We baked the dusty spool
of tape, to reverse
the degradation,
to reattach the oxide
make them playable again.

Now awake, the fledglings sit,
awaiting obsolete release
on the Tree of Lost Causes,
glowering.

The Girl Who Learned to Speak Raven

Every day of the lockdown they came
to the back of the house
at the same time of day,
a pair of ravens
to the parking lot, where our car gathered grime,
to strut on the roof of the opposite block
like pirate captains
cock-of-the-walk Charlie Chaplins:
lack of traffic
tempting them into town
down from the abandoned
missile station in the hills
from the family nest we found
tucked under the arm
of a power pylon
in Mandeville Canyon.

They have a call that means contentment
the raven purr
like the dropping of a melodic
ping-pong ball
a bubbling cluck, a churr
each distinct from the other.

We tried to call them back,
clicking away with our tongues,
clumsy at first against
the softness of our palettes,
crude caws, until one of us
suddenly got the knack:
you found a voice
they turned their heads towards.

Slowly the cars came back
trains hissed in the station

kindness evaporated
and yet, they keep returning
once every week or two
not for me, I think, but to seek
the singular call
of the girl who learned to speak raven.

Amy RaascH

Amy Raasch is a Los Angeles-based poet, musician, actor, and media installation artist. Projects include album *Girls Get Cold*, animated film *Cat Bird Coyote*, solo show *The Animal Monologues*, and forthcoming music video *Weight of a Man*. Her poetry manuscript, "Why I Am Not a Gravedigger," is a 2024 Trio Award Finalist. She holds a BA from The University of Michigan and an MFA from Bennington Writing Seminars. She writes about what haunts us.

Vase with Poppies, 1886

Lilting necks & cobalt sighs
like disappointed
ladies at a dance
just shy of midnight.
I think no one is

watching, but the museum
guard reads palms. Before
his lunch break, he takes
my hand. Says, *You must
learn to paint with blood.*

A Pair of Boots, 1887

Everything I love is ugly.
Mud on flea market boots.
Grass guts. Earth-gnawed
hobnails. Broken teeth.
Slate cross born
in a storm of wall shadow.
Ash in my third eye
spells me to sleep.
I dream my painting
then I paint my dream.

A Pair of Leather Clogs, 1888

Operatic mouths spill all the latest
sunflower news. The farm table,
stabbed daily, gouges itself
laughing. The brown room
blooms with orange-gold
wounds. I sit in my mother's
kitchen chair. All year,
she waited for summer
tomatoes from the backyard
she grew up in, next to a photo
of my sister and the dog
who outlived her splashing
in a Minnesota lake.
Ceramic Pillsbury Doughboy
shaker full of salt. Coffee
hot and black. Every day,
someone would stop by to sit
at her kitchen table. Even after
the police at the door. When
the tomatoes were ready,
she'd eat them like an apple.

The Diggers, 1889

In blue jumpsuits, two diggers
bend like question marks
near a brief exclamation of trees,
brace their shovels with the weight
of their wheat-colored clogs.
Bend and brace, bend and brace
to outpace the circling birds,
wind in the jagged evergreens.

In the museum pamphlet,
a London-based "luxury workwear"
company offers *The classic French
worker's jacket in hydrone blue.* Otherwise
known as French blue.
Cobalt, Prussian,
Ultramarine –
Van Gogh whorled them all
with enough heft to exhume
this stump among living trees.

From the brochure's slick page,
a rugged, silver-haired gent
in a polka dot scarf squints
uncharted blue eyes, cocks
his coffee mug out of focus.
My brother, a builder, works
nearby but can't take time off.
I think about buying him the jacket
for Christmas, knowing it will go

perfectly with his *hydrone blue*
eyes—the impossible color
inherited from our father (six months
in the ground and I finally found
the palette!) When Dad visited me

in Venice Beach, we went to an art
opening in a converted warehouse on 4th.
Look, A – they painted 'em on pallets!

He talked about it for years.

Bill RatneR

I drink from the trough of poetry to taste joy, grief, to hallucinate, to memorialize, to remember. I'm ecstatic about my new Slow Lightning Lit book of poems, Lamenting While Doing Laps in the Lake. I flap my lips for pay in cartoons, games, movie trailers, etc., but it's poetry I love to read aloud.

The Collar

Cop stops me on my motorcycle
Harley Hummer two-stroke
looks like a chopper
rides like a toy.

You were doing sixty in a thirty.
Township road ringed by soybean fields
I'm gonna take you in.
I try and figure out the shape of my mind

a hollow dripping with mystery
monkey mouth
I take off my helmet—cop stares
there are bones on his sleeve

razor wire unsprung
chain gate hung open
his face dances a virus
blue, a slurry of ink.

He's going to take me in
he's waiting for me to rebel.
I want the world to see I have not broken,
Well, I breathe like Sal Mineo in *Rebel Without a Cause*,

Then I'll just have to go along with you.
He's confused, like he's dropped a wrench
like he's with family. Say something, Dad.
He raises his arm like he's wiping the map

of all that is evil and wrong
Go on, get the hell out of here.
I kickstart the Harley.
Sounds like my neighbor's walk-behind mower.

Fairground

Thrill ride noise, sky gray from agri-smog,
dangerous playground equipment,
a see-saw that could break legs,
walking on asphalt hosted by Hell,
no orange poppies to guide us,
the woods my mother, the desert my father,
half-lost in industrial haze.
Some fiddlenecks are visible, and baby poppies.
Otherwise, nothing but green hills.
Drought delayed by atmospheric rivers dumping more rivers,
fueling non-native invasive species,
some poisonous, leaving no room for others to grow.
Will they bring in Monsanto? Tanks and bombs?
Who will be left to make jalapeño poppers, crazy nachos?
The Veterinary Rehab Trauma Center
warns that animal germs can make you sick,
don't put things in your mouth.
I wash my hands for twenty seconds.
Goats pant in square barred cages,
legs brown with fur,
one with his ass in the air, the other nuzzling his flanks,
dressed in a red sleeveless shirt,
their names are Low Rider and B-a-a-a-rbra.

Funeraria

They sent my mother to her grave with no
jewelry. She didn't have much.

    A cameo of her mother's face
    or maybe it's Venus de Milo
    on a brooch of Sardonica shell.

A gold plate purse ashtray
shaped like a tiny fry pan
with a paste emerald on top.

    Her Depression-era wedding band
    diamond the size of a fingernail
    clipping.

They should have buried her with amulets and silver snakes
    but instead they burned her in her dandelion color nightgown
        and lay her ashes in a white cardboard box
            that my father held in his lap on the airplane
                like a cake.

Unconsecrated in Perugia

On the steps of the holy cathedral a security guard raises his arm,
E chiuso. Non e consecrato, mi dispiace.
A decree has been penned, he says.
The Church of San Francesco al Prato has been unconsecrated—
now a godless vault stripped of adornments, absent of chalice,
liborium, and threads from the cassock of Saint Francesco.
For now, souls will idle unprotected here.

In the nave below the altar,
alongside the funerary monument of Geminiano Inghirami
rests a granite gray 715 horsepower V-12 Ferrari *Purosangue*
which now occupies the chapel just long enough
for this eight-speed dual-clutch Italian masterwork
to be made immortal in a TV commercial.

The axis of the church forms the cross, the shape of a human—
the narthex the foot, apse the head.
The shadow of a priest flutters through in a liturgical Roman cape
clutching his mitre. The stage crew adjusts lights,
car executives weigh costs, photographers charge their batteries.

Devotees are drawn to this stone-built shrine in spiritual pursuit
and prayer. The *Purosangue* with its prancing horse badge
and signature red-painted valves
does zero to sixty in 3.2 seconds.

As the moon rises the west door is locked.
Seminarians and novitiates creep
across the marble floor in ankle-length robes
secreting flagons of black plum.

One by one they run their fingers along its chrome,
stroke its leather haunches, mount the luminous four-seater
and commence a bestial, boxerless romp.
Hairless caresses, skin sliding, damask shredding,

sex, drugs, and rock & roll black mass.

As the next day dawns the decree expires.
Purosangue is summoned to its car hauler.
Relics, crucifix and sanctuary lamp
are returned to their places.
Celebrants glide across the tabernacle
darkened in spirit and pray for mercy.

Georgia San Li

Georgia San Li is currently reading *Hopscotch* by Cortázar. She has been re-reading Ishiguro, Le Guin, and Woolf. Her recent poetry was longlisted for the 2024 London Magazine Poetry Prize. Her chapbook *Small Galaxies for Breakfast* was a semifinalist for the 2024 Tomaž Šalamun Prize. She is an alumna of the 2024 Bread Loaf Writers' Conference in poetry and translation.

Jonquil

in floriography this belongs to
a genus of Narcissus,
with colored corona symbolizing
desire, renewal, often a permutation

of creativity and rebirth, a French name
for a split-level café on
Newbury, with mirrored prisms
mounted along the wall

like a glass river,
a mosaic: a clutched hand, a green
purse strap, the phallus
machinery for espresso, the beret

of a barstool, a cup of cardamom
latte topped with leafy
foam, two half-faces, introverts
peering into themselves

Elegy for the Fairy Wrens

   —after Ursula K. Le Guin

   One day long into the time channels my voice will reverberate in texta operating a disturbance, an offbeat interpolation.
   It is not a rainbow extant from the ice age, nor is it obsidian compressing a universe of galaxies by the billions, sometimes a phenomenon
      that occurs through the lens of theorems.

Texta must skip to connect with the htrae no snamuh, even if
         your texta moves in tandem
      or sideways. Watch for deathly dark cores
or defiant choruses. Dart through both joys and treacheries in tango, take on
         new formations and open
   spacing for a neo-texta to drop its scent along the belly of the belly and find your way forward.

   Tune your gesticulations to detect low decibels,
following the tip-toe traces through canals and ventricles, averting
      destruction of the evanescent. Remind the htrae no snamuh that
         movement is part subconscious sounding, learned
      through the lineage of distant
   cousins, coded through anima and star rock, texta
by texta until you are standing
      still with your palms open and tasting it
   before you swallow.

The Taxonomy of Being Desire

    –after Graham Greene

There she is, what she wants, that
Desire, less Pearl S Buck more

The Good Earth, more Jane Goodall,
more holding the rough hands of gorillas less

Juliet, more Dame Judi Dench,
less or maybe more Lady MacBeth,

more Crouching Tiger, Hidden Dragon
skittering over treetops, more delight, and

I Wonder as I Wander by Langston
Hughes, and yet Who am I? With my

back to the painter, yes, more Helga,
sprawling, more laden with longing

on a hill like a spider listening to its
web, the vibratos glistening, ping

ping! With no line of sight to what is that
impermissible Catholic despair, questioning God,

woe to such forbidden feeling, falling
from Grace that will fling

you to hellfire in the name of
The Power and the Glory – who

will answer the door but that child
again, whose church will be there and knock?

The Smithsonian BookDragon

She scans the flaps
in her fly-over, assiduous and
efficient in detecting the fire, the ice,
all-too-familiar pandemonium,
not even one passing gesture toward
complex beauty buried alive in the rock piles,
the tableau studded with tedious, middling
existences, distortions stiffened with hair spray.
Yawning at the piteous suffering, her eyes involuntarily close
shut to black out piles of prettily dull performances,
the déjà vu dystopian plot lines. She makes no
crimped corners to mark
fascination, plants no flags on
planets of discovery. Her toenails grow long
and claw into her slippers, the books left pristine,
typeset in Garamond, the spines slowly disintegrating,
porous, and crackling in dried glue and stitching, unopened,
she adds turmeric to her milk, still wanting
for something more than
the usual qualms, the usual inflammations.

June StoddarD

June Stoddard has found joy and friendship in words since childhood. She is a writer, poet, and editor. Her work is published in Muleskinner Journal and Blue Sky Press' Home, and Love Letters. June performs her work live at Slow Lightning Lit, the Rapp Saloon, at Library Girl, and the Women Who Submit Quarterly open mic. June is a graduate of UW-Madison with a double Major in English & Theatre.

My Action Figure

My friend, Patricia,
became an animated action figure.
She lived on chlorophyll.
Her voice charmed all who heard it.
Gentle caring, nurturing order,
we Skyped as she aided me
to clear, declutter, and breathe.
Patricia the action organizer
dutiful, loving, martyred.
Loving her men so much
she forgot to care for herself,
or was it the chlorophyll.
A vision of green in my veins
Made me think
Did Roundup do her in?
The healing nectar she so loved?
Did waves of pesticides spread
from field to field affecting
the potion nurturing her blood?
Did her blood turn green?
I'd never seen anyone
drink as if they were a plant
emerald flowed from her brown bottle
always by her side
I choose to believe it saved her.
Patricia lives forever in
an animated action life.

Hideout

Great Aunt Helen brought chickens to the lake
Great granddad built the chicken coop
Honing with treasured tools from Scotland
Every inch into place for his love
Between artful bending canoe staves and gunwales
Stretching canvas watertight to ferry chickens
Did they only eat the eggs?
Or was there an end of summer chicken feast?

Long after chickens and greats were gone
Slatted leaky roof, pine needle floor
Became my dilapidated playhouse
The built in tree trunk held up the roof and open door
The legless chair and rough lichen covered table
Where imaginings found a home
A fort, a castle, a pirate's den
Lookout peep-holes to protect
From slanted shadows
In the great-grands' chicken coop
Where mother placed golden MacIntosh Toffee
In the roll top treasure tin trunk.

Predominant Poise

Great Aunt Junie was a transplanted Southern Belle,
a Fox Chapel horticulturist in beefsteak begonias,
whose bearded leaves grew to the size of a head.

In my wraith youth we shared a breakfast
on rosebud plates with egg cups for soft boiled eggs,
on toast with homemade marmalade.

While we overlooked her terraced garden,
a pair of miniature dachshunds awaited a crumb.
Junie's blue eyes appraised me
"You have such grace"
I didn't think I did, living in
a NYC cockroach infested tenement.

Smooth empowering words,
like the silken slips given out to nubile nymphets,
which I was at twelve,
grown to twenty-three she advised me
 "Hold your power"
As she had, marrying well twice.
"Never let men touch you."

Of course, by then it was too late.

Nancy Lynée Woo

Nancy Lynée Woo is an eco-centric poet who harbors a wild love for the natural world. In 2015, she was an Emerging Voices Fellow with PEN America. Her MFA is from Antioch University and her first book of poetry is called I'd Rather Be Lightning. She loves and appreciates the warmth of the literary community.

Signs of Life

Nothing seems to matter
as much as the Laysan albatross
feeding plastic to its young.
Parents skim over the surface
of the sea for fish, beaks scooping
up lighters and zip ties
that they pass on to their chicks
whose underdeveloped gullets
can't expel the trash.

Thousands of miles from any
human establishment,
small decaying bodies dot the shore
of the remote island,
leaving a pile of bottlecaps behind
in a mound of feathers.

It's the green feet of the coot
through my binoculars
that keep pulling me back
to the bedside of the great mother
floating in a jar at the beginning of life.
I feed her my sorrow
and she says, *Look, child—*
over there—a rustle in the bushes—

suddenly, the sparkling orange
breast of a western bluebird
swerving above my head—

Self-Portrait with Clouds and Worry
    —after Eduardo C. Corral

I'm a messy bed and a half-filled
        notebook. I'm 106 journals
in the closet. I'm protection oil
        and a yoga studio, flip-
flops in the basket, bike out front.
        I'm coming out of the sewer
with my lips flapping. Pitchfork
        in hand, I'm flipping
the compost, digging for worms.
        I'm flying to Seattle,
taking the ferry, mushrooms
        on tongue, laughing
hysterically at the emerald forest.
        I'm waiting for the hurricane
to pass. I'm texting everyone I know.
        It's raining. It's flooding.
It's 110 degrees in Portland
        and wildfire season
in Vancouver. I'm on the train,
        in the sky. I'm eating
mango in Mexico, learning French.
        I'm in the mountains,
snow boots on, kale and white bean
        soup on the stove,
dog leash in hand. I'm hiding
        from myself, I'm overthinking
everything. I'm going crazy.
        My friends are sane, at least.
I'm an anklet on my sister, a zipper
        on the skin. I'm a summer
of beaches, a table of paintings,
        a stereo in the living room.
I'm no longer blinds withdrawn.
        I'm acrylic on canvas,

cleaning videos on YouTube.
    I'm rearranging the furniture
and digging myself out of anger.
    I've never been this old
before. I've left youth behind,
    saying what I think
to the man I love. I'm walking
    up the hill with a basket
of troubles, reveling in nonsense.
    The clouds look ominous.

Listen

> —after W.S. Merwin

I learned to carry the weight
of others. Then I learned
to put it down. I don't know

if unraveling ever ends,
or if it's supposed to
but I'm saying actual thanks.

Thank you, onion growing
in a pot, dishes drying, down
comforter, luxury of crying.

In a shared garden bed, we grow
peppers, tomatoes, squash, rows
of strawberries waving tiny arms.

Bleak though it is, we have

    grass, fence, weeds

    music, soup, candles,

    books, blankets, lights,

    each other in our lives.

Guy ZimmermaN

Zimmerman is a playwright and theater director linked to Padua Playwrights, currently living in earthly bliss in Irvine, and teaching in a writing program at UCSD. He enjoys long walks with Duchamp among others, and celebrates starlight.

The 68 Dreams of the Tantric Trucker

1.

He was the only white guy
corn rows ever looked good on,
the secret prince of Wales.
It was part of his signature ghetto look.

2.

The Siberian Ice Maiden
has a vision three hours before she dies.
You are thinking of it now.
The vision is actually a premonition
of Bernini's Saint Teresa—
alter course accordingly.

3.

During his acid trip in Death Valley
Michel Foucault is pierced by a vision.
You are already seeing it.
You realize now Foucault's vision
channeled Ernst Haekel's paintings
of the kind of undersea life once populating
Death Valley. Revise accordingly. (if necessary, immediately)

4.

On a moonlit night
the hungry dog from the sculptor's poem
has wandered into a human structure.
Don't focus on the structure
but on the dog's body and face,
her eyes and mouth.

5.

A figure is there with food for the dog.
Your body tells you who it is.
A woman has brought food for the dog.
She is tall and carries a valise.
Play close attention to the fabric of her coat.

6.

Sometimes she puts on a pair of panties
that belonged to an old lover and stands
looking at herself in the bathroom mirror,
her hand looped down between her legs.
In her mind she sees the lover dancing.

7.

Diane Sawyer dreams
about walking through the Rothko chapel
but it's different and like a forest.
A panther arrives.

8.

At dawn the host of soldiers
on horseback and elephants
approach the line of trees
that mark the border of Sakya.
There the old Gotama sits,
eyes open, in mediation. Like him
you see the mayhem and bloodshed to come. Draw it.
A hummingbird visits the old man
and, hovering in the air,
becomes something different.

An Equation

A fused rib ripped from the back of a clipped bird: wishbone.
The still raw crook of it convenes a council of signs
on the kitchen sill.

Plus, plus, plus, dark saint of inventories,
small headaches and mice,
prancing its iron crown across yellow tiles,
collecting seconds like the spores of maggots
singing out its vain "Sieg-heil!"

And minus too works silent in the slim bone shadow,
subducting drizzled blood and small last feathers,
festooning fresh bird bone with a white
stiffness.

The wish-rib engenders next
the X magician, ancient crux of calculation,
hard as stone hauled from the heart of a cold orb,
spinning furious in the X-void.

The dead X-eye beneath the bone arch toes a line across the glaze,
adds snake-eye dots on either side,
releasing one last quotient rush of hen-remembrance:
the sun in spastic dance around the dimming yard,
the jerks of brief and headless flight above seed-stewn
loose dust.

To the disregarded bird
such acrobatics total less than
or equal to the blur of the farmer's hatchet,
greater than or equal to the collected weight of clouds
above Nebraska on the pre-selected afternoon.

But the wishbone dries on, stiffens into itself,
preparing a death-cry

for the caged stoat of life-longing
who weaves the infinity sign --let me go! let me go! --
until its gem-sized heart explodes
with nothing left to settle the issue but a quick
pinky tug.

Wake

That thing where any statement becomes poetic
just like death might arrive from any direction and love
is just the other side of knowing. Myself crossing
Houston Street with dust and shards of glass,
a sacred residue, baking in summer heat.
For men, you said, nostalgia is the only safe form of feeling.
Don't do it. Don't reach for that cell phone.

Everyone is a poet now except you, but no one
will accept your denials and everything you say
turns out to rhyme in a tasteless way and nobody
remembers how to sleep or even what sleep is.
Do not imagine falling forward into cushions of light.
I have never held you. I am not holding you now.
Also, I have never believed all the slander, the broken words,
the stories of your cruelty, your endless thirst.

Black widows bedeck the patio furniture, dozens of them,
and you are training them for neighborhood races.
So much has become habitual. Ashes fill my cup.
Along my thigh you run your fingers, so close, so charismatic,
one eye patched, the sutures popping off as they surface
along your arms. In your one eye the great dark whale
thunders up toward the sun.

So, you want to rule the world? That is like climbing a tree to look for fish.

                 -Mencius, Warring States Period

Jeremy RA

Guest Editor
SLANT 3: Folio Edition

Jeremy Ra is a queer, Chinese-Korean-American poet living in Los Angeles. A Best-of the-Net and Pushcart nominee, his poems have appeared in Spillway, I-70 Review, Cultural Daily, among others. He was a twice-finalist for the Steve Kowit Poetry Prize and the recipient of the Morton Marcus Poetry Prize. His first chapbook, Another Way of Loving Death, was published by Moon Tide Press, and his collaborative chapbook, God Is a River Running Down My Palm, was published by Picture Show Press. He is the co-host of the video series, Poetry.la.

Peggy DoBreeR

Poet
Editor-in-Chief
Slow Lightning Lit

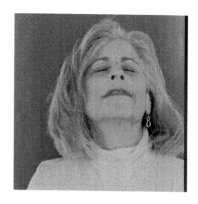

Slow Lightning Lit
Daily Somatic Writing Practice

"WHERE MINDFULLNESS MEETS THE MUSES" *Slow Lightning Lit began in search of the whimsical and miraculous in a darkening world, in January, 2021.* Guided embodied meditation practice and prompted writing in exquisite community online, out of which publishing and fine literary events are imagined. Curated by former dancer, award winning poet, and poetry advocate Peggy Dobreer. All are welcome, memberships for those who stay. www.slowlightninglit.com

www.slowlightninglit.com

Slow Lightning Lit Titles

Slow Lightning III: Folio Edition
2025

with Jacinta Camacho Kaplan, Celia Chavez, Esther Cohen, Mandy Rae Hartz, Loraine Despres, Peggy Dobreer, Darothy Durkac, Janet Fitch, Ruthie Marlenée, Roberta H. Martinéz, Murray Mednick, Andrew Nicholls, Colleen O'Mara Diamond, Simon Petty, Amy Raasch, Bill Ratner, Georgia San Li, June Stoddard, Nancy Lynée Woo and Guy Zimmerman

Lamenting While Doing Laps in the Lake
Bill Ratner 2024

Living Poetry
Murray Mednick 2024

As Man Is to God: A Poem on the Making of Werner Herzog's "Fitzcarraldo"
Andrew Nicholls 2024

Slow Lightning II: Astonished Poetry
2024

Slow Lightning I: Impractical Poetry
2022

You don't jump in front of the lines, you are awake behind them.

-Murray Mednick, *Living Poetry*

Made in the USA
Middletown, DE
17 February 2025